9 + 5 = 14

9 + 4 = 13

9 + 8 = 17

17

13

9 + 3 = 12

9 + 7 = 16

9 + 6 = 15

9 + 5 = 14

9 + 9 = 18

9 + 7 = 16

9 + 6 = 15

I Like to

frac

Disney's

Doug's™ Word Book

Created by Jim Jinkins

by Liane B. Onish
Illustrated by Nick Pietropaolo
and Tony Pietropaolo

Doug Funnie, age 12 1/2

New York

For information address Mouse Works, 114 Fifth Avenue, New York, New York 10011-5690.
Printed in the United States of America.
First Edition
10 9 8 7 6 5 4 3 2 1
For more Disney fun visit www.DisneyBooks.com
ISBN: 0-7364-0021-4

CONTENTS

A
Smash Adams

Beebe Bluff
B

Cleopatra Dirtbike
Funnie
C

Doug
D

Edwina Klotz
E

Funnie Family
F

Guy
Graham
G

Hamlet, Patti's guinea pig

Imagination

Judy

Miss Kristal

Lucky Duck Park

Patti Mayonnaise

Neematoad
N

MAN O STEEL MAN
Man-O-Steel Man
comics
O

Porkchop
P

Quailman
Q

Roger Klotz
R

Mr. Swirly's
Mr. Swirly
S

Theda Funnie
Doug's Quailman Underpants
POWER BRIEFS CHARGER
Skeeter Valentine
X ray
Wacky Wizzer
Fentruck is from Yakestonia
KlotZilla

The Funnies are an average, middle-class family . . . even though they named their new baby Cleopatra Dirtbike Funnie.

Phil Funnie, Doug's dad, is the Busy Beaver Department Store baby photographer.

Judy Funnie, Doug's older sister, goes to the Moody School for the Gifted because she is so talented.

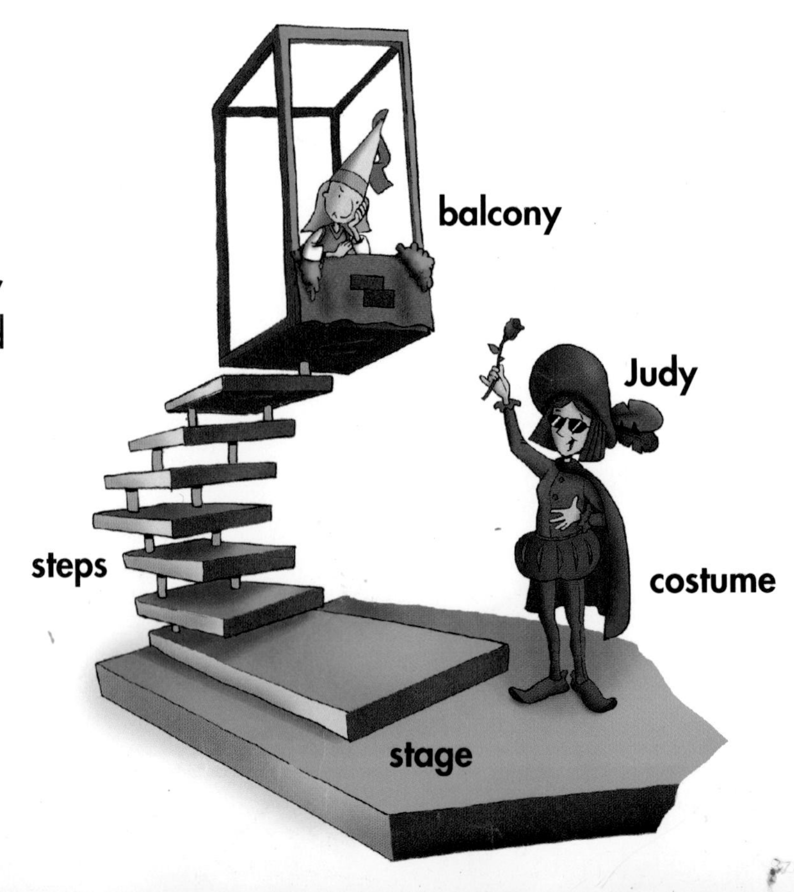

Grandma Opal is adventurous. Sometimes she drops in unexpectedly.

DOUG'S FUNNIE HOME

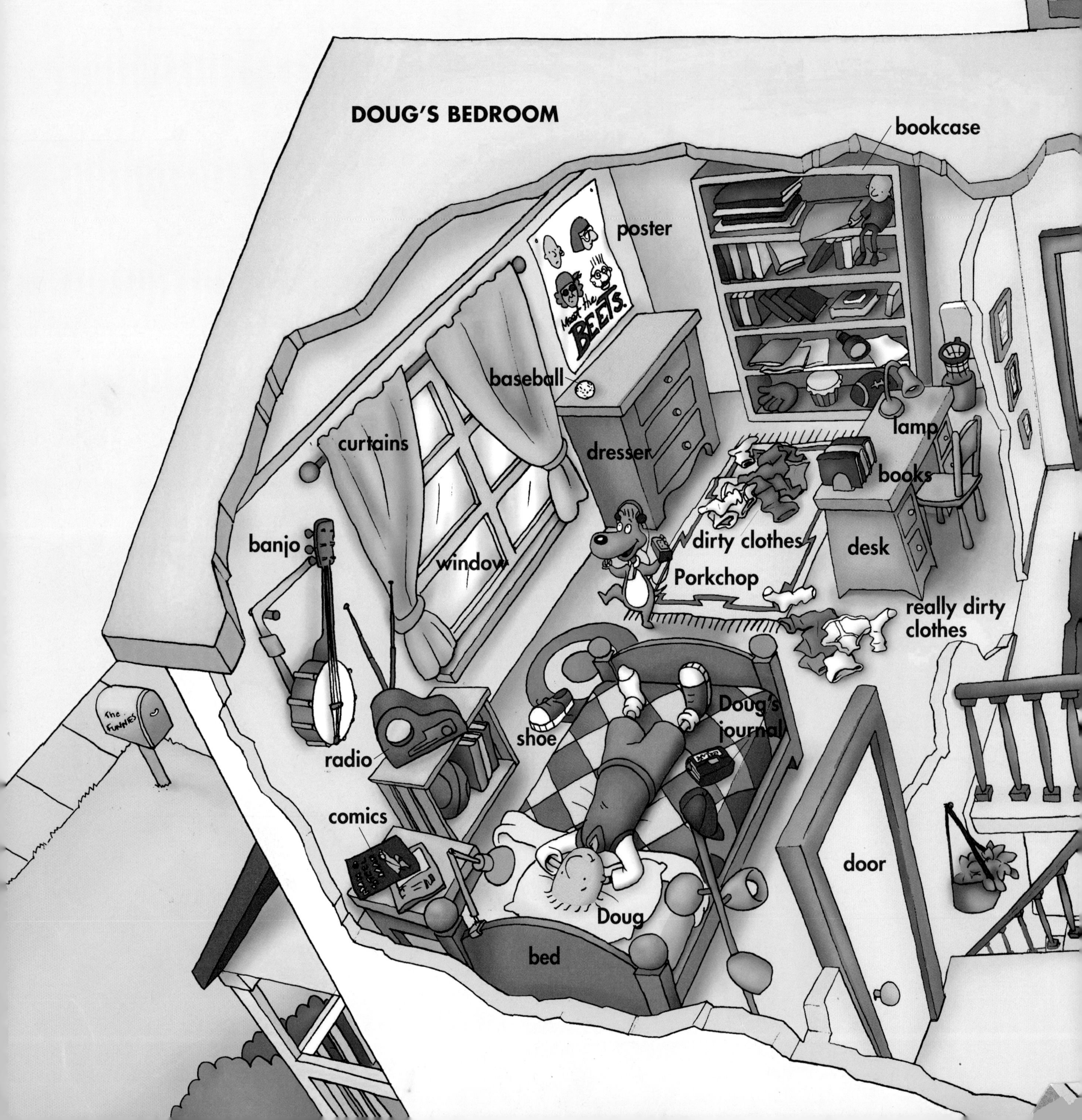

Doug and his family live at 21 Jumbo Street, in Bluffington.

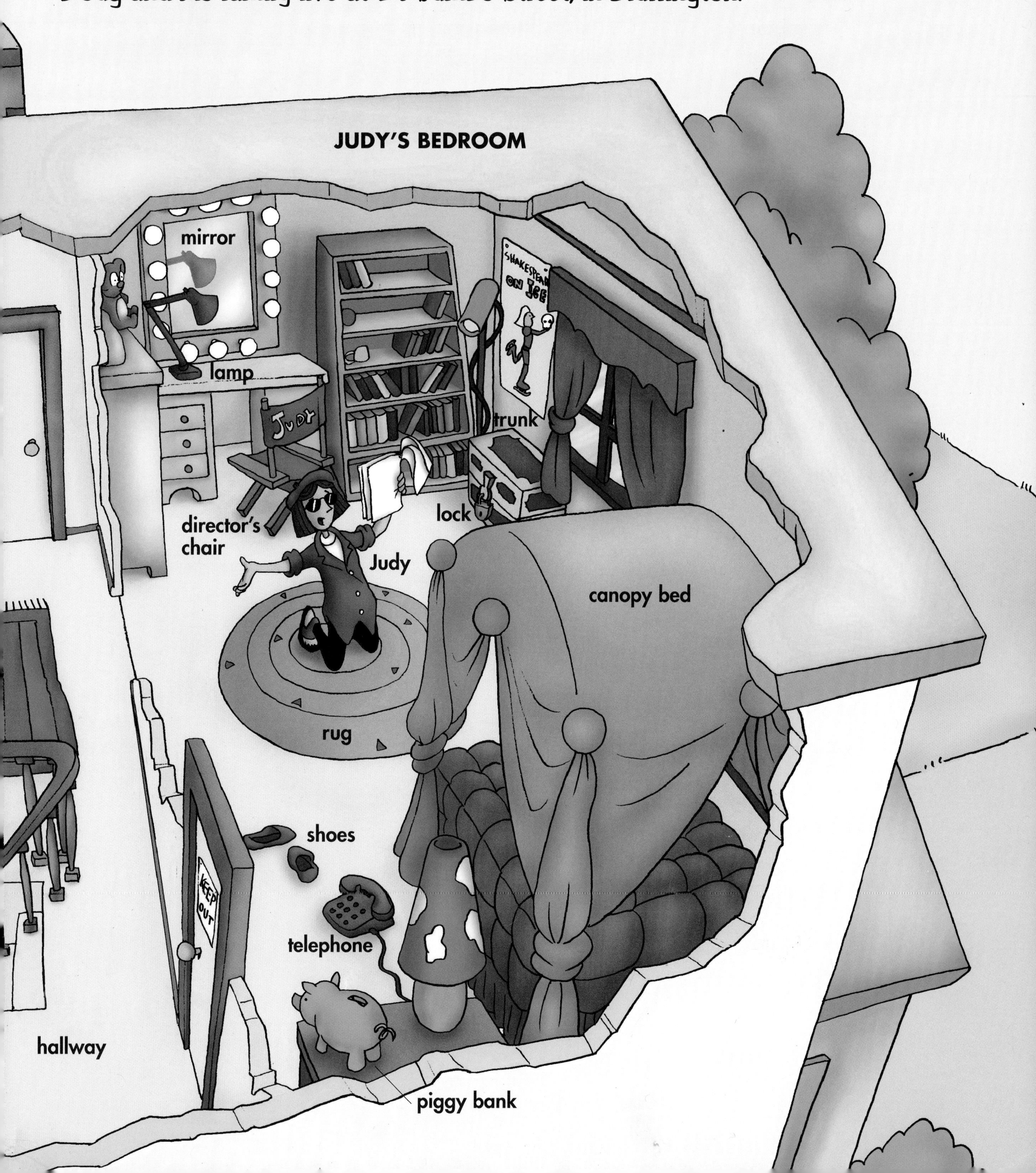

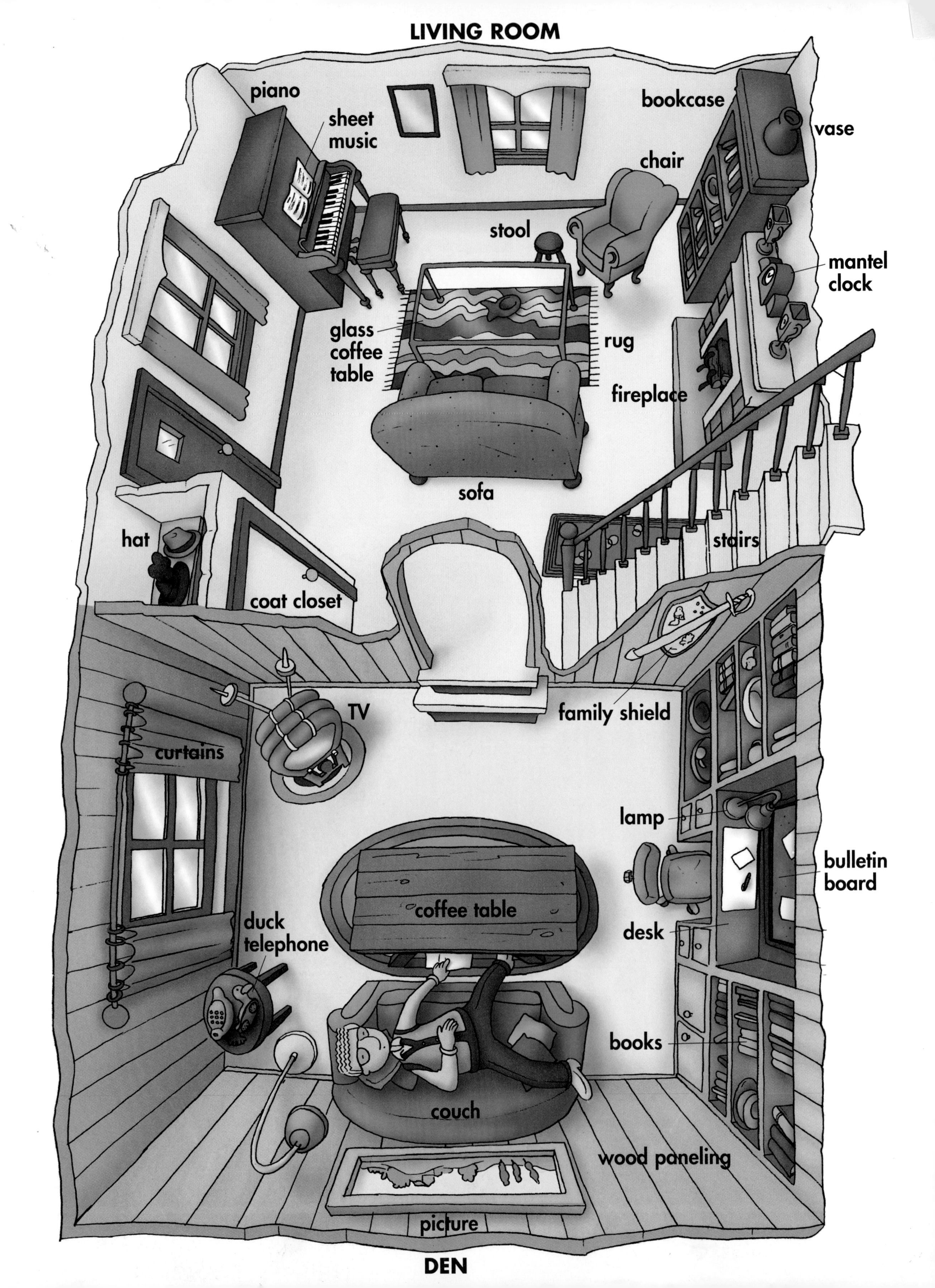
LIVING ROOM
piano
sheet music
bookcase
vase
chair
stool
mantel clock
glass coffee table
rug
fireplace
sofa
hat
coat closet
stairs
TV
family shield
curtains
lamp
bulletin board
coffee table
duck telephone
desk
books
couch
wood paneling
picture
DEN

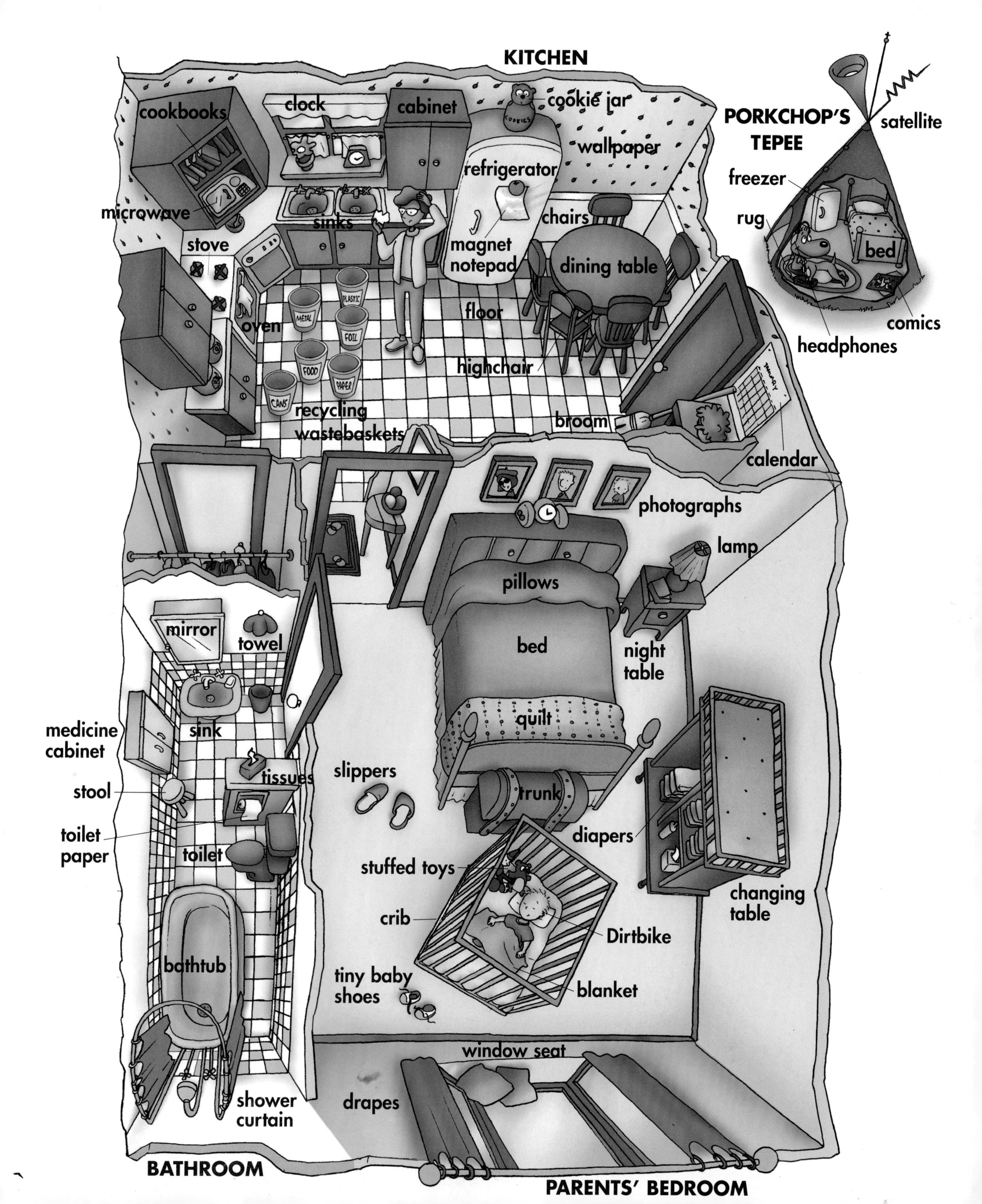
KITCHEN
cookbooks
clock
cabinet
cookie jar
wallpaper
refrigerator
microwave
sinks
magnet
notepad
chairs
stove
dining table
floor
oven
highchair
recycling
wastebaskets
broom
PORKCHOP'S
TEPEE
satellite
freezer
rug
bed
comics
headphones
calendar
photographs
lamp
pillows
bed
night
table
quilt
trunk
diapers
changing
table
mirror
towel
sink
medicine
cabinet
tissues
stool
toilet
paper
toilet
slippers
stuffed toys
crib
Dirtbike
blanket
tiny baby
shoes
bathtub
window seat
drapes
shower
curtain
BATHROOM
PARENTS' BEDROOM

DOUG'S IMAGINATION

Doug likes to imagine that he is Quailman, a superhero from the planet Bob. Quailman, with his best pal, Quaildog, do good and battle scary stuff.

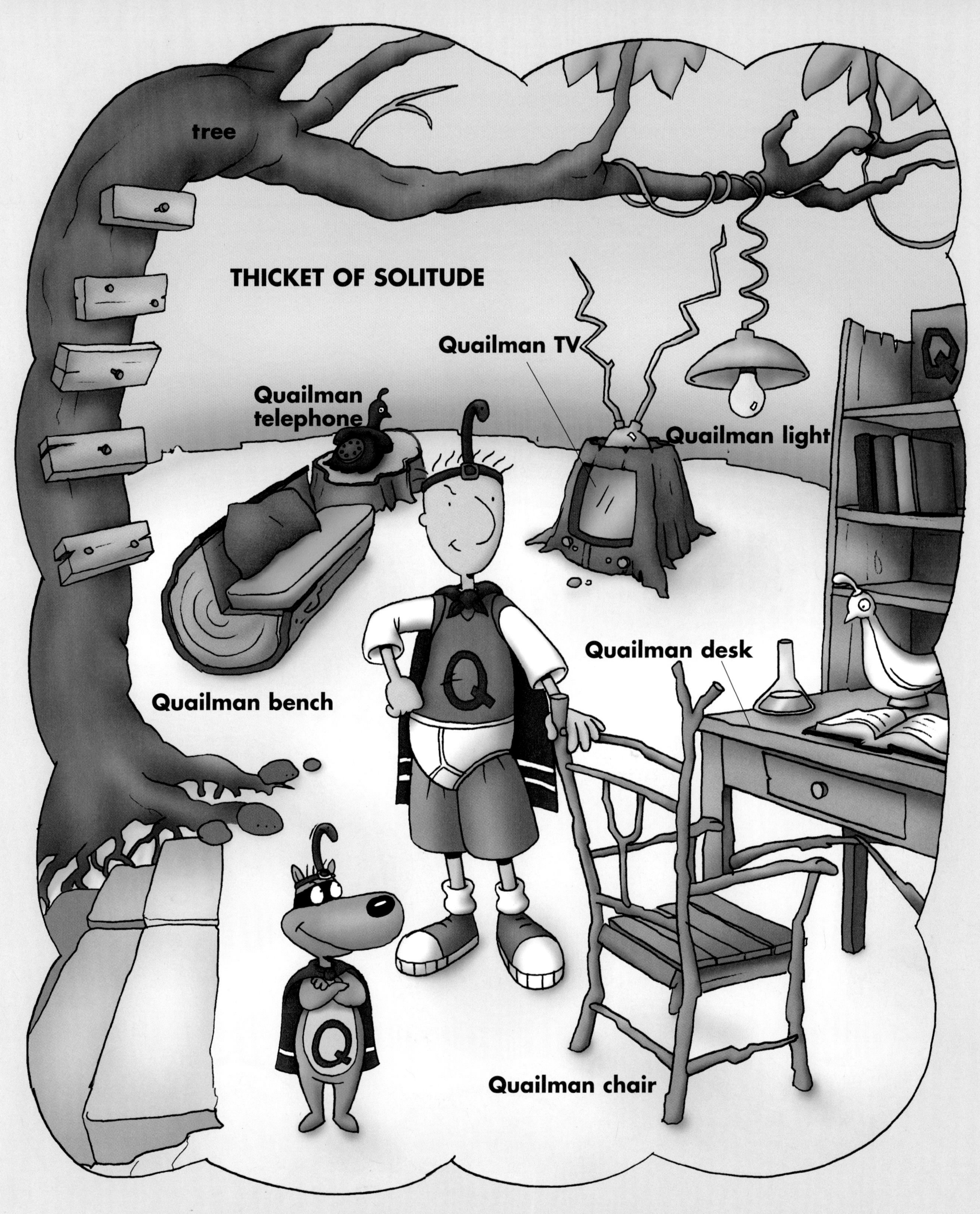

When Quailman and Quaildog are not busy battling scary stuff, they like to spend time in their secret hideaway, the Thicket of Solitude.

Sometimes, Doug wishes he were his favorite adventure movie hero, Race Canyon. Race Canyon senses danger before it happens, narrowly escapes every disaster, and wears a really cool hat. Doug, as Race Canyon, always gets the prize.
Nice outfit, kid.
the real Race Canyon
Doug as Race Canyon
brown jacket
cool hat
brown pants
really high cliff
boots

At other times, Doug imagines himself as Smash Adams, star of comic books and movies. Smash is a superspy secret agent.

DOUG'S FRIENDS, NEIGHBORS,

Skeeter Valentine, Doug's best human friend, is really cool and really smart. He likes to invent stuff but usually it's not very useful.

AND ROGER, TOO
Chad Mayonnaise, Patti's dad, has been confined to a wheelchair since a car accident.
girl
Patti Mayonnaise, Doug's secret love, is cute, popular, a natural athlete, and a born leader.
Patti's pet guinea pig, Hamlet
bike
wheelchair
Roger Klotz likes to say he's rich, R-I-C-K-H.
bully
money
leather vest
cat
Stinky, Roger's cat, is Roger's closest, and maybe only, real friend. Stinky hates Porkchop.
man
Roger's dad is a clown. He visits, but not often.
clown hat
woman
comb
Edwina Klotz, Roger's mom, is a hairdresser at Rose's Beauty Parlor.

Bud and Tippy Dink, Doug's next-door neighbors
Bud is the headline writer for the *Bluffington Gazette*.
Tippy is mayor of Bluffington.
cell phone
GUIDE FOR MAYORS
magazine
expensive gadget
baseball cap
football
Connie Benge, Doug's friend, likes playing loud punk rock music. Porkchop likes to play, too.
speaker
music
guitar
basketball uniform
volleyball
running shoes
Chalky Studebaker, Doug's friend, is the best athlete in school and gets the best grades in the whole class.
Porkchop

Mr. Sleech experiments with new cookie recipes in his basement.

Al and Moo Sleech are twin ten-year-old geniuses. They attend the Moody School for the Gifted.

Beebe Bluff, Doug's friend, is so rich she has a TV that fills a whole wall in her bedroom and gets a bazillion channels. She is secretly in love with Skeeter.

Bill Bluff, Beebe's dad, owns Bluffco Industries, Bluffington's largest employer.

Betty Bluff, Beebe's mom, helped raise money to build the beet-shaped water tower.

DOUG'S NEIGHBORHOOD

The playground is just down the block from Doug's house.

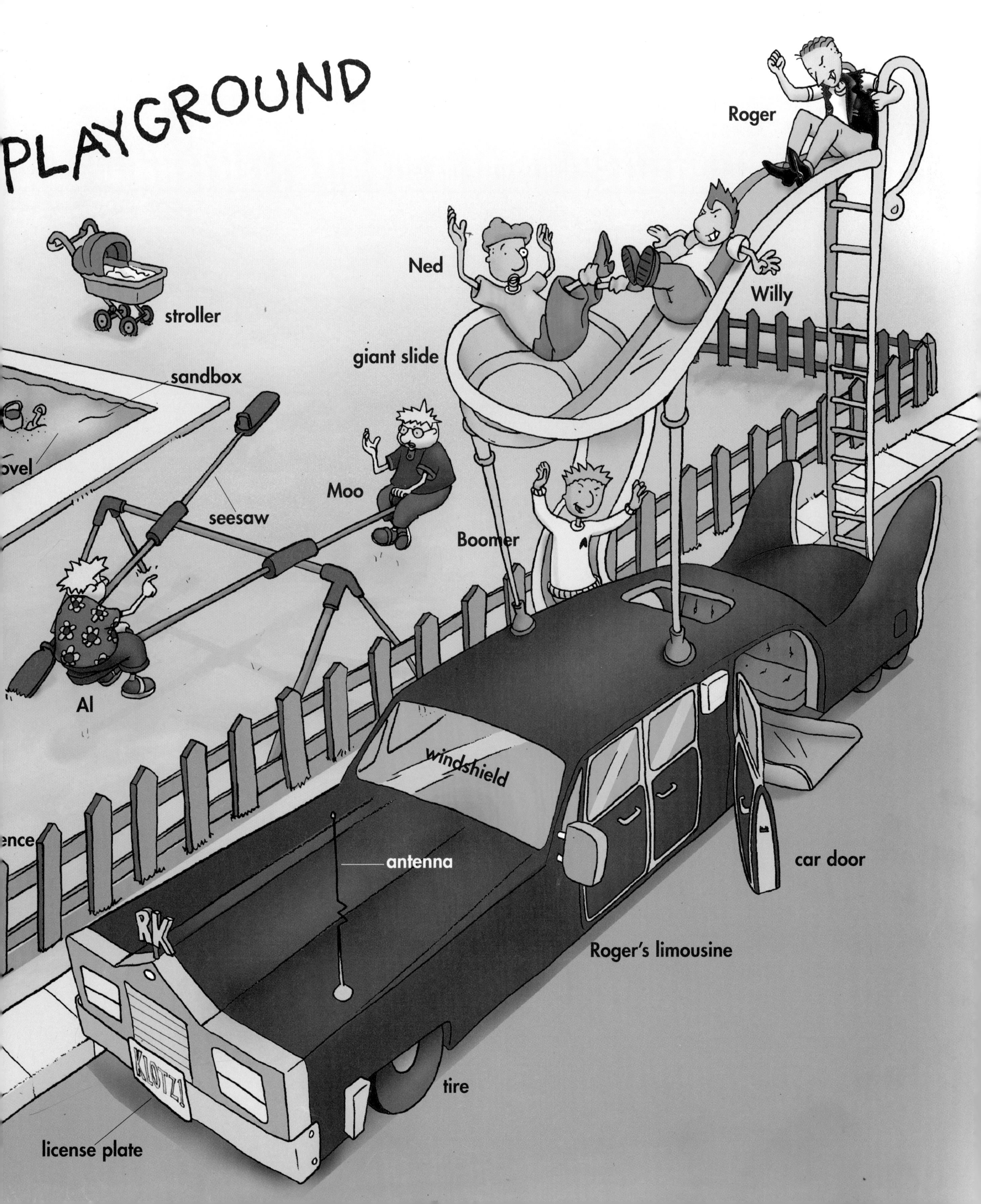
PLAYGROUND
Roger
Ned
Willy
stroller
giant slide
sandbox
ovel
seesaw
Moo
Boomer
Al
windshield
ence
antenna
car door
RK
Roger's limousine
KLOTZ1
tire
license plate

LUCKY DUCK PARK
kite
bleachers
Wacky Wizzer
150
beet mitt
beet-ball
third base
beet-ball bat
pitcher's mound
beet-ball diamond
home plate

Patti's Pulverizers practice on the beet-ball field in Lucky Duck Park.

LUCKY DUCK LAKE

At the bottom of Lucky Duck Lake
in Lucky Duck Park lurks the Lucky Duck Monster.
No one has ever seen the monster, but Doug and Skeeter keep trying.

airplane
bronze statue of
a Neematoad
bushes
splashing
wading
picnic blanket
picnic basket
thermos
pretzel
ants
Swiss cheese
hot dogs

DOUG'S SCHOOL

Doug goes to the new Beebe Bluff Middle School. It's not so bad going to a school shaped like a friend's head. Just don't think about the fact that science class is in her nose.

MISS KRISTAL'S ENGLISH CLASSROOM

Miss Kristal really brings literature to life!

BAND ROOM

Doug practices the banjo and dreams of winning Patti Mayonnaise's heart as a rock and twang star. Bob Fort is the music teacher and marching band director. Boy, is he tough!

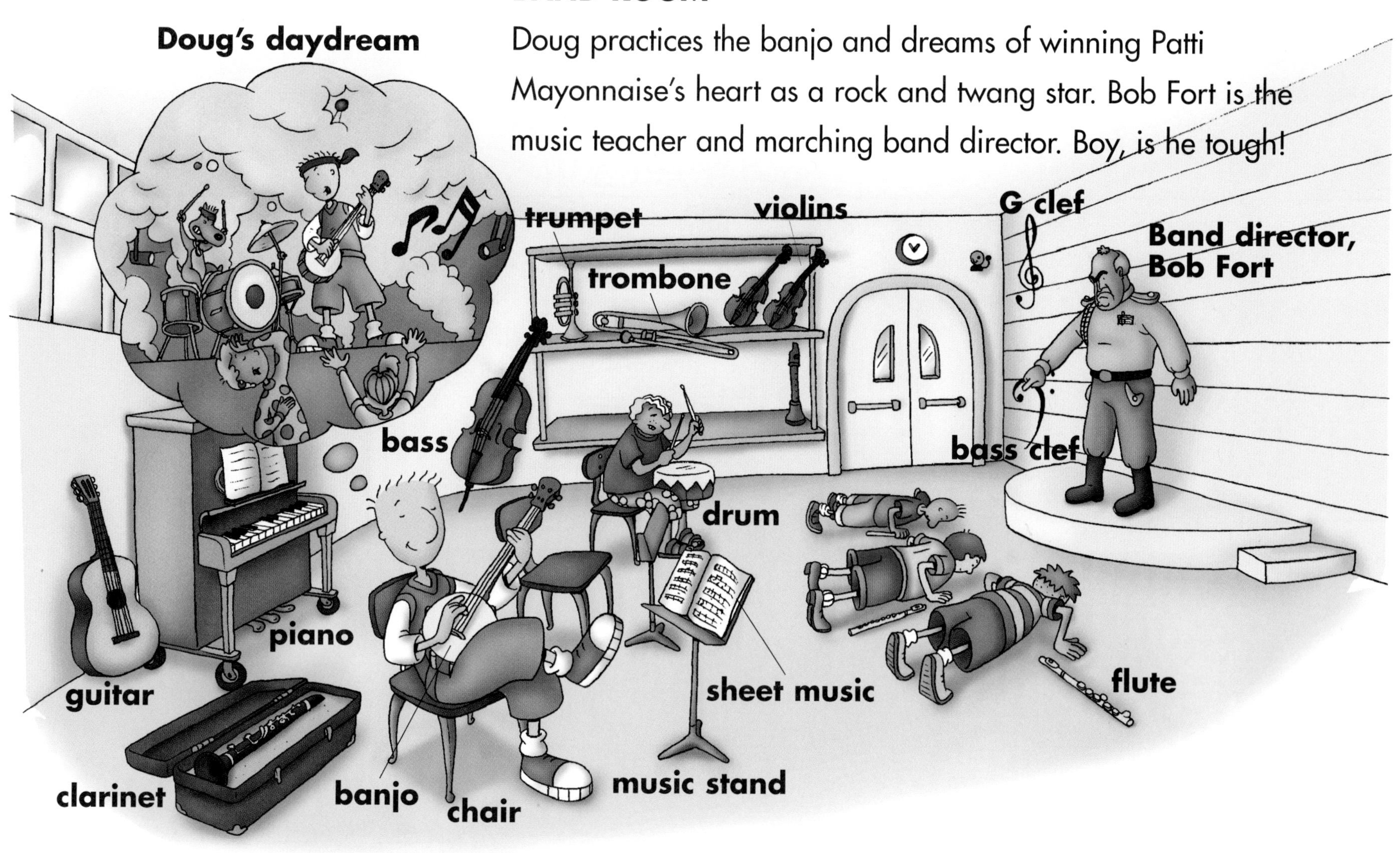

METAL AND WOOD SHOP

The Heaver Twins teach shop. Homer Heaver teaches wood shop. His twin brother, Road Heaver, teaches metal shop.

PRINCIPAL BOB WHITE'S OFFICE

THE *WEEKLY BEEBE* OFFICE

Guy Graham is an eighth grader and runs the *Weekly Beebe*.

LUNCH BARN CAFETERIA

GYMNASIUM

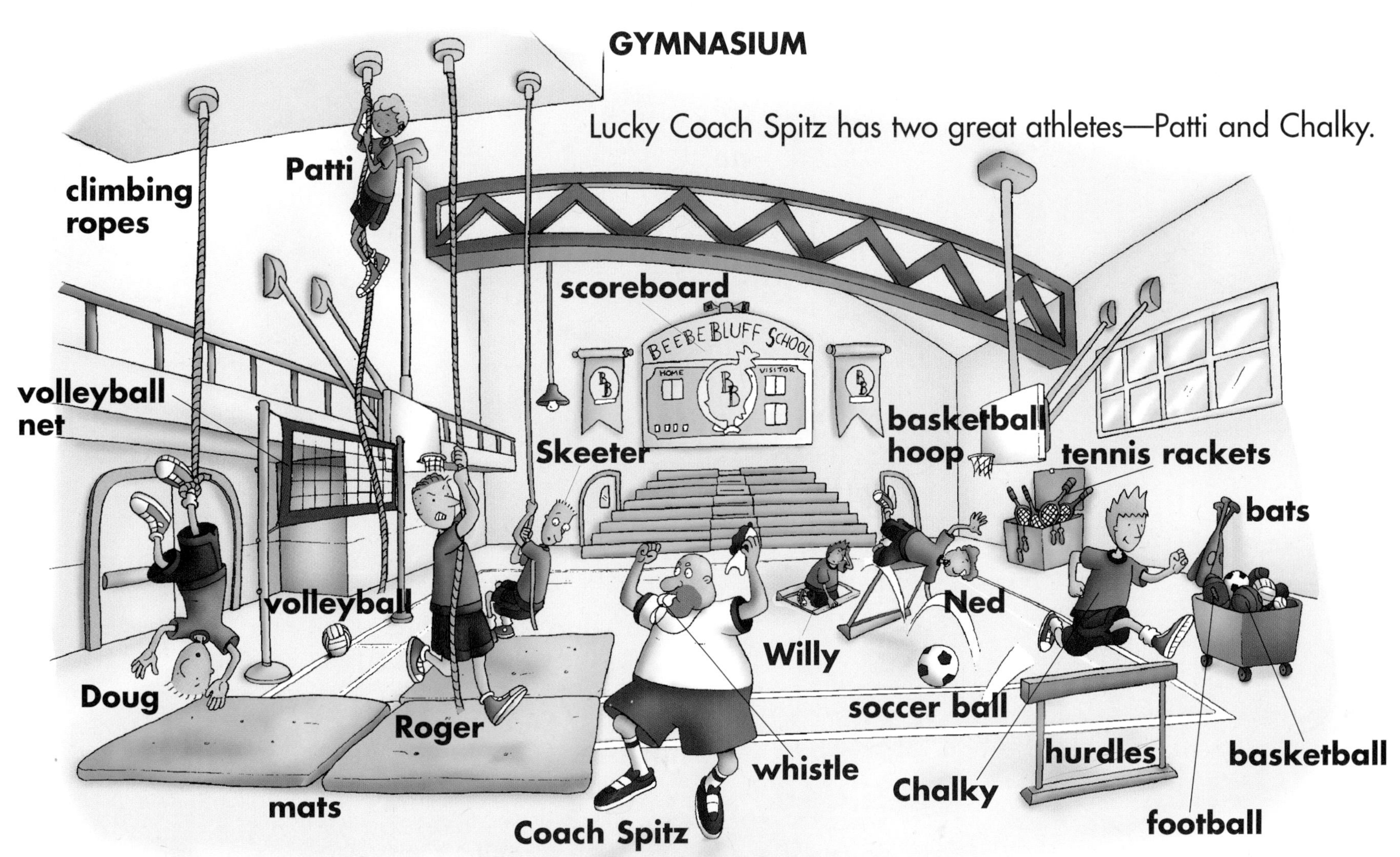

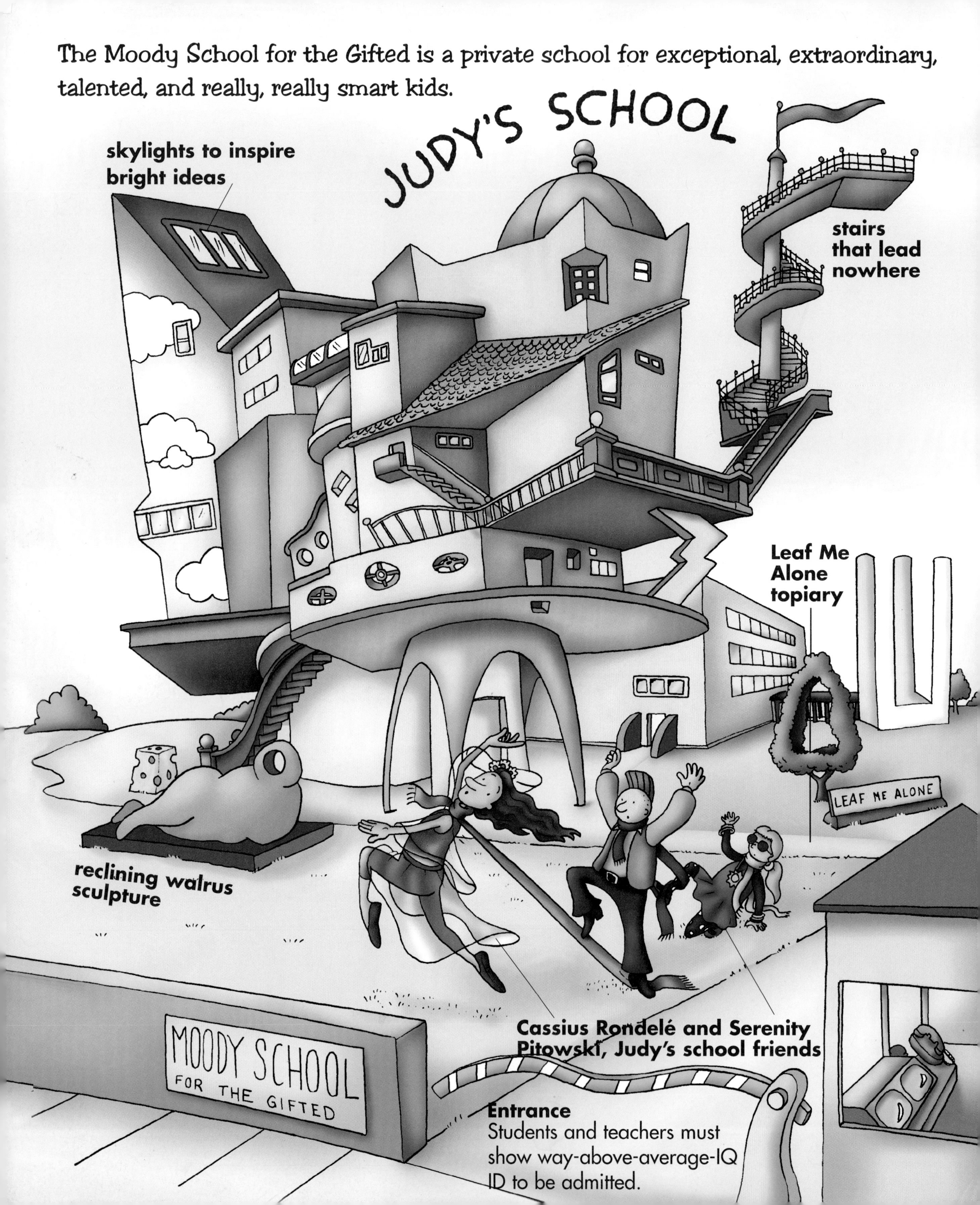
The Moody School for the Gifted is a private school for exceptional, extraordinary, talented, and really, really smart kids.
JUDY'S SCHOOL
skylights to inspire bright ideas
stairs that lead nowhere
Leaf Me Alone topiary
LEAF ME ALONE
reclining walrus sculpture
Cassius Rondelé and Serenity Pitowski, Judy's school friends
MOODY SCHOOL FOR THE GIFTED
Entrance
Students and teachers must show way-above-average-IQ ID to be admitted.

THE MOODY SCHOOL FOR THE
GIFTED SCHOOL THEATER
balcony
props
stage lights
director's bullhorn
Theater in the
Nearly Round
stage stairs
Judy Funnie,
director
seats
light board

DING DONG DAY CARE
Three-year-old Dale Valentine, Skeeter's little brother, likes to spend many happy hours demolishing the Ding Dong Day Care Center. Doug hopes Dale doesn't completely destroy Ding Dong before Dirtbike is old enough to get her first taste of school.
DING DONG DAY CARE
plants
pots
little chairs
blocks
Architecture 101, Leaning Tower of Beet
toys
sand table
tricycle
wheel

funny hats
shade
mop
cot
dress-up
corner
broom
cubbies
ittle table
class pet iguana
easel
clay
finger paints
apron
Neematoad
costume
story rug
books

The Mr. Swirly Ice Cream Factory and Soda Shop is one of Doug's favorite places. It's a great place to hang out and, hopefully, see Patti Mayonnaise. Unfortunately, Roger and his gang also hang out there.

Chalky Studebaker works out a complicated game play. Fries score!

MR. SWIRLY'S
Swirly
menu board
table
Mr. Swirly's colossal two-foot-tall Brain-Freeze Cone
Mr. Swirly's Kitchen Sink Sundae
counter
stool
tray
Roger's gang
Skeeter
booth
Peanutty Buddy Cone

The Bluffington Scouts, Troop 671, is led by Doug's neighbor Mr. Dink. The scouts learn many useful skills, such as squirrel calling, logrolling, and snake tying, and earn merit badges, too!

Skeeter earned his second merit badge in squirrel calling.

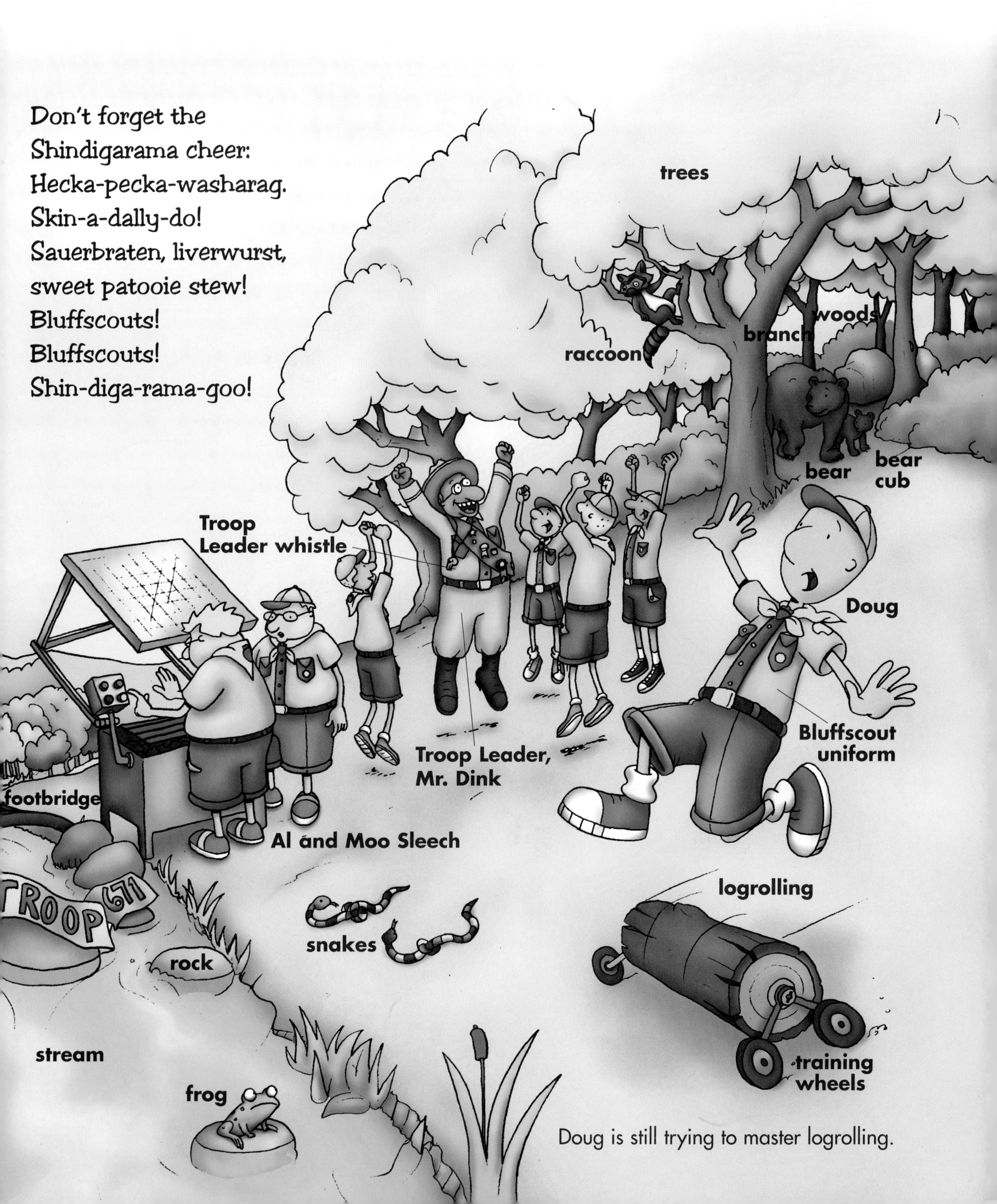

Doug is still trying to master logrolling.

BLUFFSCOUTS CAMPING OUT

After a busy day, Bluffscouts Troop 671 sets up camp.

Doug's tent
big tent
yak-hide tent
cot
inflatable tent
cups
pickled beets
cans of beans
plates
picnic table
spoons
sleeping bag
bicycle pump
Porkchop's tent
PORK CHOP
cooler filled with milk
BUG JUICE

The Bluffscout's Favorite Camping Treat:

STICKY GOOEY BEETY TREATS

2 roasted marshmallows
1 chocolate bar
2 Graham Crackers
2 Pickled Beets

Place chocolate bar on one graham cracker, top with roasted marshmallows and pickled beets. Cover with the second graham cracker and BON Apetit!

671
very big tent
gadgets
LATRINE
tools
shovel
indoor shower
(never used)
campsite
tent poles
hot dogs
solar panels
marshmallows
mallows
water
faucet
graham
crackers
popcorn
campfire
chocolate bars

DOUG DAYDREAMS

Doug daydreams about what he'd like to be when he grows up.

Dear Journal, when I grow up I'd like to . . .

. . . be a handsome cowboy at home on the range. Patti Mayonnaise would *have* to be impressed.

. . . be the astronaut who discovers intelligent life on a distant planet. I bet Patti Mayonnaise would be impressed.

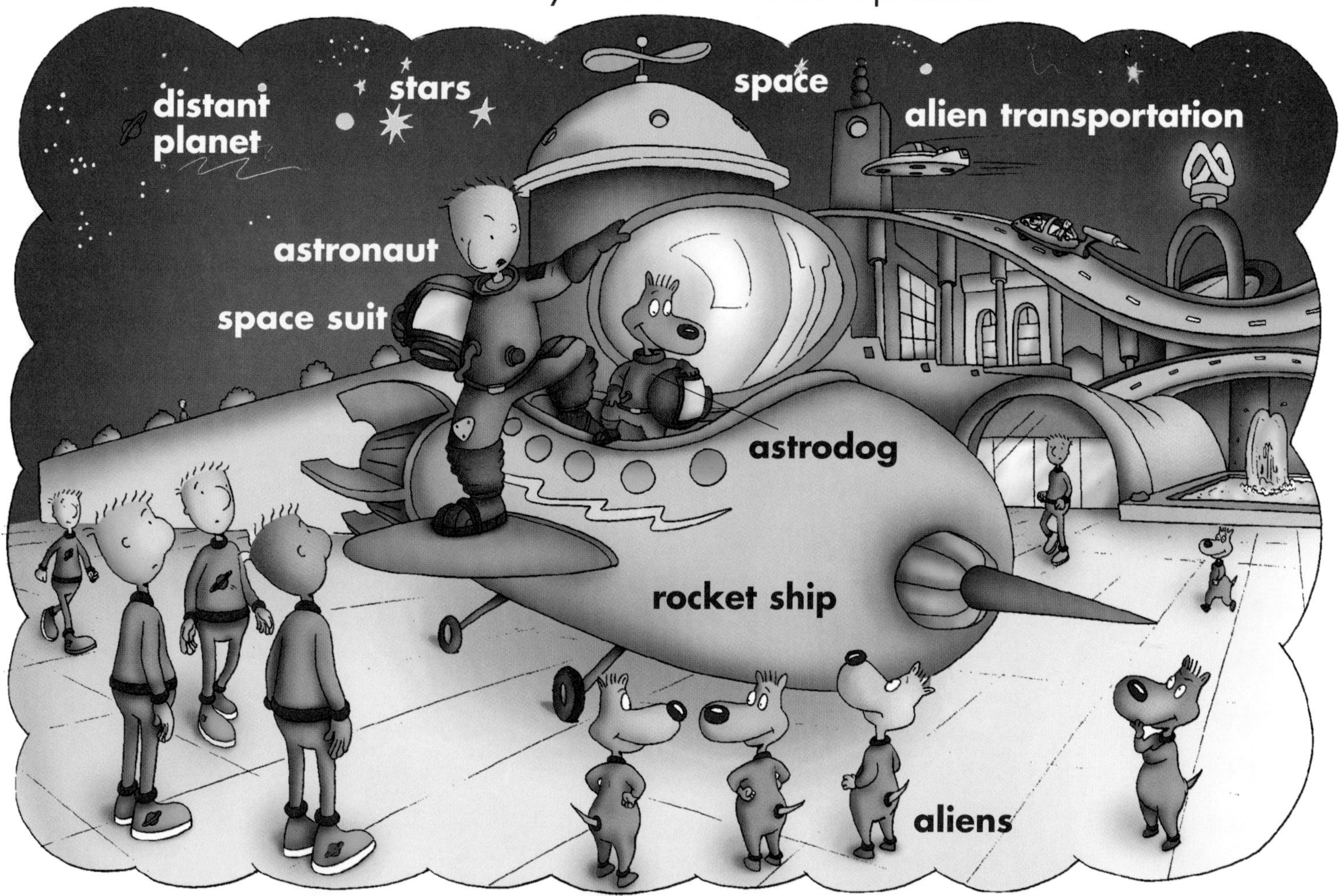

. . . be the archaeologist who finds the prehistoric cave paintings of the primitive humans who first lived in Bluffington. I bet Patti Mayonnaise would be impressed.

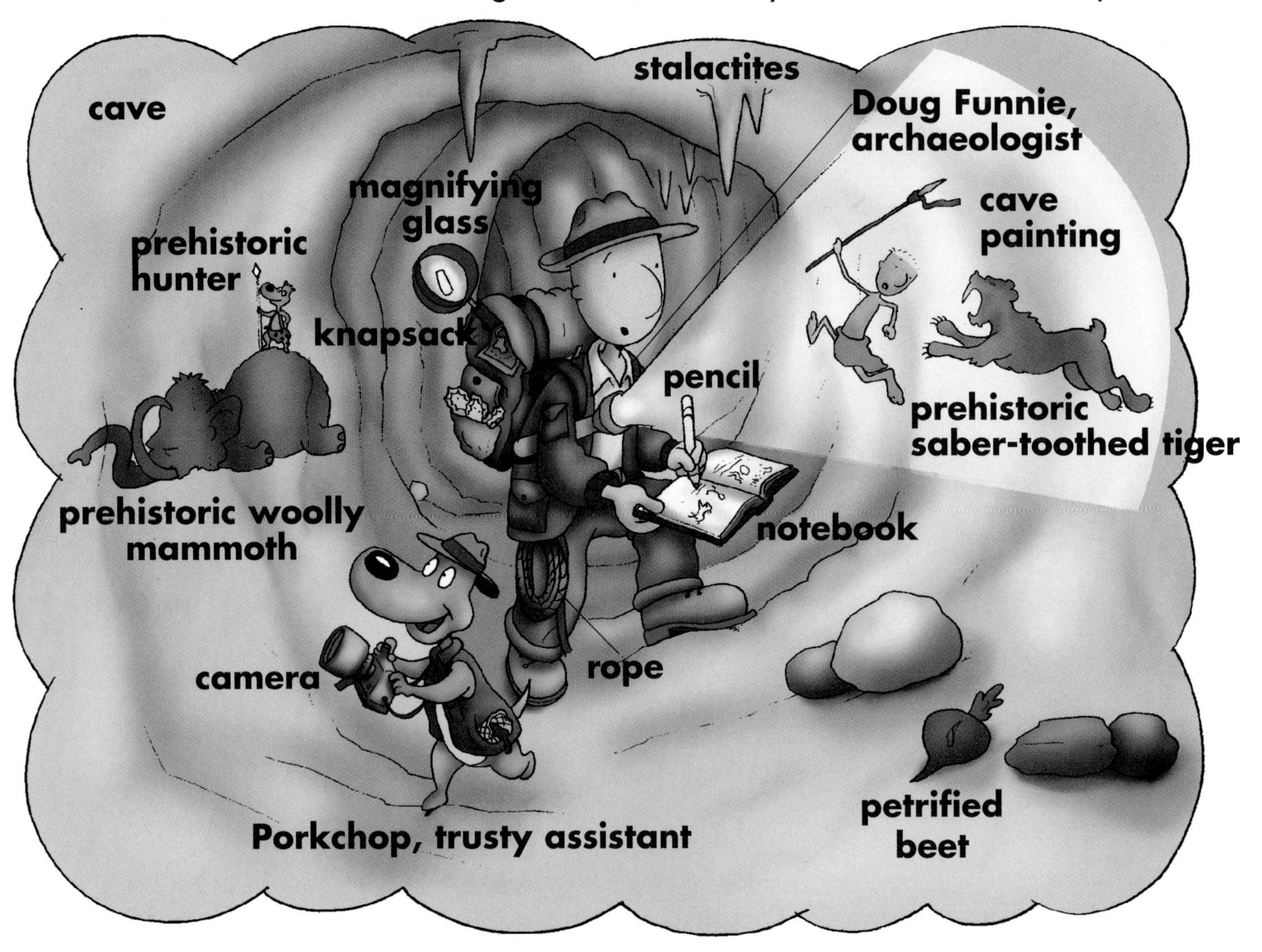

. . . be a famous cartoonist. I bet Patti Mayonnaise would be impressed.

. . . be the firefighter who rescues Patti Mayonnaise from a burning building! Patti Mayonnaise would be happy.
Patti Mayonnaise
helmet
smoke
Doug Funnie, firefighter
crowd
turnout coat
hero
boots
ladder
fire hydrant
water
fire truck
fire
hose
burning building

DOUG'S WORLD

Hope you enjoyed your tour of Bluffington!

Four-Leaf Clover Mall

Beebe Bluff Middle School

Mr. Swirly's

Mr. Dink's house

Doug's house

Bluffco Industries

water tower

BLUFFINGTON

Doug Funnie

Founder's Hill

Doug's best nonhuman friend, Porkchop